BETWEEN PANCHO VILLA AND A NAKED WOMAN

(Entre Villa y Una Mujer Desnuda)

By

Sabina Berman

Translated from the Spanish
By Shelley Tepperman

NoPassport Press

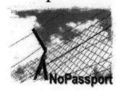

Between Pancho Villa and a Naked Woman/Entre Villa y Una Mujer Desnuda) by Sabina Berman

Volume copyright 2014 by Sabina Berman
Play copyright 1993 by Sabina Berman.
Translation copyright 1997 by Shelley
Tepperman

NoPassport Press
Dreaming the Americas Series
PO Box 1786, South Gate, CA 90280 USA
NoPassportPress@aol.com, www.nopassport.org

ISBN: 978-1-312-62614-0

NoPassport

NoPassport is a theatre alliance & press devoted to live, virtual and print action, advocacy and change toward the fostering of cross-cultural and aesthetic diversity in the arts.

NoPassport Press' Dreaming the Americas Series and Theatre & Performance PlayTexts Series promotes new writing for the stage, texts on theory and practice and theatrical translations.

Series Editors:

Randy Gener, Jorge Huerta, Mead Hunter, Otis Ramsey-Zoe, Stephen Squibb, Caridad Svich (founding editor)

Advisory Board:

Daniel Banks, Amparo Garcia-Crow, Maria M. Delgado, Elana Greenfield, Christina Marin, Antonio Ocampo Guzman, Sarah Cameron Sunde, Saviana Stanescu, Tamara Underiner, Patricia Ybarra

NoPassport is a sponsored project of Fractured Atlas. Tax-deductible donations to NoPassport to fund future publications, conferences and performance events may be made directly to http://www.fracturedatlas.org/donate/2623

Between Pancho Villa
And a Naked Woman

A Play

By

Sabina Berman

Sabina Berman is a playwright, storyteller, essayist, and film and theater director. She is one of the most prolific and daring writers within her generation and in the Spanish language. Her work deals mainly with the issue of diversity (human and animal) and its obstacles: the striving for domination, with its derivatives (authoritarianism, violence, discrimination). Her style features humor and irony, the distrust of all official discourse, subversion, the need to go beyond both sexual and theatrical boundaries, and the use of language itself. She is a four-time winner of the National Playwriting Award in Mexico (Premio Nacional de Dramaturgia en México) and the Juan Ruiz de Alarcon Award (Premio Juan Ruiz de Alarcón). She has twice won the National Journalism Award (Premio Nacional de Periodismo), in 1999 and 2007. Her plays have been staged in the Americas, and her novel *Me* (*La mujer que buceó en el corazón del mundo*) (*Moi* in French) has been translated into 11 languages and published in 33 countries. In 1995, she was co-director of the film *Between Pancho Villa and a naked woman*, with Isabelle Tardan. She also wrote and co-produced the film "Backyard", which represented Mexico at the 2010 Oscars. Recently, she wrote the film *The History of Love* for **Alfonso Cuarón** and *Light* for Alejandro González Iñarritu.

CHARACTERS

GINA, 40-ish
ALBERTO, 45
ISAAC, 25
PAULINA, 42/ WOMAN
PANCHO VILLA

GINA doesn't have to be extremely attractive, but she must be the kind of person one would immediately like to have for a friend. She has a pleasant, charming manner and tends to reconcile the people around her. If in these pages she loses her good judgement rather frequently, becoming brusque or doing foolish things, it is because she has been subjected to extreme circumstances.

ALBERTO doesn't have to be especially good-looking either, but he should be the kind of person any woman would want to invite to dinner to see whether he really is as sensual as she suspects underneath his somewhat dour and crusty exterior. He has the calculated unkempt stylishness so common among sophisticated intellectual types, and is mesmerizing to listen to. He can suddenly become "possessed" by politics and speak quickly and feverishly.

PAULINA is a forthright woman. She resembles former Mexican President Plutarco Elías Calles in both her gestures, her face, and her intelligence. This in no way implies that she is not attractive—Plutarco was an extremely handsome man! Paulina has both physical charms and a highly entertaining sense of irony. She is, of course, an ideal partner for any undertaking that requires energy and determination.

ISAAC is a well-built young man. Around Gina he stutters, sighs, and stares languidly, but with any other mortal he displays a confidence that occasionally even tips over into insolence He usually wears worn jeans, running shoes, and a silver earring in his right ear.

VILLA is the mythological Pancho Villa straight out of Mexican films from the 1950s, 60s and 70s—or the Hollywood Westerns from the 30s, 40s or 60s (e.g. *Villa Rides*.) Perfectly virile, with an extraordinary ability to suddenly turn violent or sentimental. He speaks with a "Hollywood Mexican accent."

WOMAN, 40-ish (played by the actress playing PAULINA) is a daughter of the Mexican aristocracy. She speaks with an "upper crust" Mexican accent.

Note: Except where indicated, American actors should not perform with accents.

Time: the present (mid-1990s)

Locations:

1 - An apartment in Mexico City's "Condesa" neighbourhood.

Within the apartment:

• A somewhat bourgeois living room with at least the following   elements: large windows, a sofa, a low table, and a stool. The main door to the apartment faces onto the living room, and there is easy access to the bedroom and kitchen.

• A bedroom.

2 - The entrance to an apartment building.

ACT ONE

SCENE 1

PAULINA and GINA are having tea in the living room.

GINA   Every two or three weeks.

PAULINA   Two or three weeks?

GINA   Or four of five days.

PAULINA   Uh huh.

GINA   It depends.

PAULINA   On what?

GINA   Sometimes he's out of town.

PAULINA   Uh huh.

GINA   Did I tell you he's writing a book?

PAULINA   Really? On what?

GINA   Pancho Villa.

PAULINA   God! Just what we need. Another
            book about that macho
            gunslinger.

GINA   Anyway, he always phones
            before coming over.

PAULINA   How considerate.

GINA   (lights a long, black cigarette) He
            says: I'm a few blocks away—can
            I come over? Or: I'm at the
            university, I need to see you. Or:
            I'm in the phonebooth at the
            corner, will you let me in? I
            always let him in.

PAULINA   Uh huh.

GINA   I open the door—we have a
            certain ritual. I open the door, he
            stays on the threshhold and just
            looks at me. He looks at me...
            then, he comes towards me: he
            kisses me. (She touches her lips.)

PAULINA   <u>You</u> don't kiss him.

GINA   No. I need a minute—or two or
            three—until something—
            something clicks—until the
            feeling comes back from memory.
            Then I bury my hand in his hair
            and... it's only then that they
            open.

PAULINA   That what open?

GINA   My lips. The cream. I forgot the
            cream. *(She exits, carrying her cup.)*

PAULINA   Her lips. I wonder which ones?

The doorbell rings.

SCENE 2

*GINA opens the door. ALBERTO, wearing a beige
raincoat worn from about ten years of loving use, is
leaning against the door frame.
They look at each other. ALBERTO squeezes
GINA'S waist and kisses her on the lips as he pulls*

her toward the bedroom. A few moments pass until
her right hand rises to his hair and buries itself
there. When they reach the bedroom ALBERTO
scoops GINA up in his arms and carries her over
the threshold.

SCENE 3

PAULINA   Straight to... to the bedroom. Ah.
               That's what you call a man who
               likes to get right to the point.
               (*Gina returns with the creamer.*)
               Although I'll bet once he's in the
               bedroom he doesn't always hit
               the mark.

GINA   Oh no, when he's inside he's...
               (*she pours the cream slowly from
               about 8 inches above the cup, slowly
               creating a long stream.*) Once he's
               inside, he's—

PAULINA   Errr. That's enough, thanks.

GINA   Divine, Paulina. Inside, he's
               divine.

PAULINA   So, what's the problem?

GINA   It's just that every time he comes, he—

PAULINA   I should have known, when he comes.

GINA   <u>Here</u>, to my apartment.

PAULINA   Ah, to your apartment.

GINA   Everytime, before we make love... we always get into the same ridiculous fight. Him trying to get me right into bed, and me trying to drag him into the living room for a cup of tea.

PAULINA   Do you want to get married?

GINA   To him? No. No. *(She laughs.)* No. *(Serious)* No.

PAULINA   Because he's already married?

GINA   No. Even if he weren't. Really.

PAULINA   So, if you don't want to marry
            him, why bother with the living
            room?

GINA   I want to have a cup of tea with
            him. Damn, I forgot my tea. *(She
            exits, carrying the tea service.)*

PAULINA   *(After tasting her tea)* Why did she
            take everything away? I've never
            seen her so strung out before.
            *(She goes after Gina, carrying her
            teacup.)* Gina...

A telephone rings offstage.

SCENE 4

*GINA enters from the bedroom, talking on the
phone. PAULINA doesn't see GINA coming and
goes into the kitchen to look for her.*

GINA   Where are you? Which airport?
            Are you coming or going?

PAULINA   *(off)* Gina?

GINA   I had an appointment. With a
                notary. So come. Come, come.
                Don't worry, in forty-five
                minutes you'll be here. Yes, me
                too. Me too. Me too.

GINA hangs up. She remains standing, breathing
deeply.
The doorbell rings.

SCENE 5

GINA opens the door. ALBERTO is in the doorway
in his beige raincoat, holding a suitcase. He stares
at her for a long time. His right shoulder is against
the doorframe. There is something vulnerable in his
expression. A beat.

ALBERTO   *(Softly, serious)* May I?

GINA   Yes.

ALBERTO   Are you sure?

GINA   Yes.

ALBERTO   I'd die if one day you said: no, no
           more, it's over.

GINA   Or if you never called again, I
           would die.

ALBERTO   No, *I* would die.

GINA   All right: if you stop calling me,
           die.

ALBERTO   All right.

(ALBERTO places his suitcase inside the door. He puts his hands around GINA'S waist and kisses her; kissing, they walk backwards towards the bedroom. After a moment GINA buries her right hand in his hair. Just before they reach the bedroom he scoops her up in his arms but GINA realizes what is happening and jumps down.)

GINA   Wait. We're going to have some
           tea.

ALBERTO   Some what?

GINA   I haven't seen you for a whole
           month.

ALBERTO   Exactly.

GINA   <u>Exactly</u>. *(Pulling away and going into the kitchen)*. So, tell me.

ALBERTO   *(Hanging his coat on the coatstand)* What? I told you: I was in Toronto. Didn't I tell you? I left a message on your machine a month ago. And I was gone a month. I taught some classes. A course.

GINA   On?

ALBERTO   On? On the history of the Mexican Revolution. So where's the tea?

GINA comes out of the kitchen.

GINA   Water takes time to boil.

ALBERTO   Oh?

GINA sits down on the sofa.

GINA   Toronto—that's in the south of
                Canada. Right near the US
                border.

ALBERTO   Near Niagara Falls.

GINA   Wow. They're even interested in
                the Mexican Revolution up there.

ALBERTO   Gina, I need to feel you... I need
                you to touch me.

GINA   Come on, sit down. Can't we talk
                for awhile, like civilized human
                beings?

                *ALBERTO thinks about it. He goes
                to sit on the sofa, but GINA puts her
                legs on it so that there is no room for
                him. Resigned, ALBERTO sits on
                the hassock. (Gina picks up a little
                silver box from the low table, takes
                out a long, black cigarette, and lights
                it.)*

GINA   So, what did you think of
                Niagara Falls?

ALBERTO   They're.... imposing, that's the
word, imposing. Literally tons of
water rushing down every
second.

GINA   *(interrupting)* I know. I've been
there. I went with Felipe, ten
years ago.

ALBERTO   *(annoyed)* With Felipe. Did you
have a good time?

The conversation has dried up.

ALBERTO   *Bending towards her.* I'm under
your spell. I dreamt about you
every night.

The kettle whistles. GINA hurries to the kitchen.

ALBERTO   Where are you going?

GINA   To make the tea. Aren't we
supposed to have tea? *(She goes
into to the kitchen)* Did you work
on the book?

ALBERTO   On the Villa book, yes. *(A beat.)*
Actually, it's going well. I've been

carrying my notes around everywhere. I was at a board meeting for the paper* and I caught myself doodling sombreros. I've got Villa on the brain from morning till night. But right now I'd like to take a break from Pancho "The Centaur" Villa, if you don't mind. (a beat) I mean, I've already started to draw up the outline of the book. But that's the boring part. I wish I was right in the thick of the story—I'd love to be on horseback with The Centaur riding to Mexico City. Villa, followed by his men—the Division of the North, galloping towards the capital. A ragtag army—a ragtag people— swooping down on the City of Palaces. All those poor starving sons of bitches coming to confront the corrupt bouregois politicians and demand what's rightly theirs. Anyway, I'll write it better than that. But let's talk about something else. Though not that much better. I'm not striving for linguistic finesse. My book won't be written with a limp wrist. I want people to feel the violence of the situation: I want my book to smell of horses, of sweat, of gunpowder. So where's the tea?

GINA   *(who has returned and is sitting back down on the sofa)* It's steeping.

ALBERTO   It's "steeping". *(Looking into Gina's eyes)* Ahh, fascinating.

GINA   How's Marta? *(An uncomfortable pause).*

ALBERTO   *(after clearing his throat)* I haven't seen her. I mean, I haven't seen her for four weeks. I was in Toronto, I just told you. *(He becomes nicer.)* I'm sorry, they're fine. I phoned Marta last night. My daughter was asleep but I'm sure she's well. I'll see them this evening, of course. Gina, I don't know why you insist on talking to me about my daughter's

mother. It—it makes me
uncomfortable.

GINA   Because Marta called me.

ALBERTO   She called <u>you</u>?

GINA   You didn't send her the child
            support for April.

ALBERTO   Yes I know, Gina, but just stay
            out of it. *(pause)* How's your son?

GINA   Fine. He was supposed to come
            back for his holidays. But he
            decided to stay in Boston to study
            for his finals.

ALBERTO   Gina, I don't live with that
            woman anymore. It's all flotsam
            and jetsam from my past. You
            believe me, don't you?

GINA   I believe everything you tell me.

ALBERTO   Well, you shouldn't. I'm
            irresponsible. I abandon what I
            love the most. I don't know why.
            (A beat.) You know that. It's
            obvious—I have two broken

marriages behind me, but you don't want to see that. You want to change me. *(A beat).* It would be easier to just trade me in for another man.

GINA   What do you think about the elections in Oaxaca?

ALBERTO   This is what you call a normal conversation?

GINA   This is what I call an easy conversation.

ALBERTO   They stole the ballot boxes in Oaxaca and there were shootouts in the street and four dead.

GINA   So then, tell me about your students.

ALBERTO   No.

GINA   Then I'll tell you how the factory's coming along.

ALBERTO   No. I'm not interested in your work. Especially when you're setting up a "maquiladora", when you're becoming part of the neo-conservative tornado ravaging this country. Those sweatshops are a betrayal of the Mexican nation. *(A beat)* Those border factories are one more symptom of this country's economic ills. They're going to turn us into another Taiwan.

GINA   We're creating jobs for people.

ALBERTO   No. You're enslaving them. And that partner of yours—what's her name?

GINA   Paulina Elías.

ALBERTO   Paulina Elías Calles, granddaughter of the supreme traitor to the revolution.

GINA   If you met her, you wouldn't—

ALBERTO   I'd kill her. Just like I'm going to kill her grandfather twenty times over in my book.

GINA   *(trying to placate him)* The point is to have a civilized conversation.

To have a natural human relationship.

ALBERTO   *(in a quick outburst)* There's nothing that's both human and natural at the same time. We're the only species of animal with a memory, therefore, with a history, with an accumulation of habit. We've been accumulating habits for about 8,000 years. Ergo: anything <u>purely</u> natural is impossible; "natural" in the sense of historically determined, as in "ingrained rote-like behaviour", is not only possible, it is unfortunately practically unavoidable.

GINA   You're impossible.

ALBERTO   Naturally. And I want you.

(quickly, overlapping)

GINA   There's nothing wrong with you wanting me just a little bit longer—

ALBERTO From the moment I left
Toronto —

GINA And me wanting you —

ALBERTO Four hours on the plane and one
in the taxi, wanting you.

GINA Calmly, so we don't —

ALBERTO Don't what? —

GINA So we don't kill the desire. Kill it
like an animal.

ALBERTO You're domesticating me.

GINA That's right.

ALBERTO Ahh.

GINA You see, we're already making
love.

ALBERTO We are?

GINA Talking, looking at each other,
desiring each other from a
distance, letting the desire
build — we're already making
love.

ALBERTO   It's just that making love from a
          distance—

GINA   Ready for tea?

ALBERTO   (*Sharply without touching her*)
          Gina. Listen. Your eyes.

GINA   What about my eyes?

ALBERTO   Sometimes they're grey. And
          sometimes green. Depending on
          the light. But sometimes—when
          your pupils are dilated, like right
          now—when they open wide like
          that... when against your will
          your pupils get all dilated, the
          gold flecks in your irises—

GINA   My what?

ALBERTO   Your irises.

GINA   Uh huh?

ALBERTO   Those gold flecks in your irises
          expand too. Like right now, as
          I'm talking to them. Your irises
          are a golden ring. A golden ring

around your fully dilated
pupils...

GINA   My irises?

ALBERTO   Your golden irises. Sometimes,
            when I'm alone and I'm tired, and
            I'm about to fall asleep, and the
            silence is weighing on me, I let
            my eyelids close and I find your
            golden eyes. And I fall asleep
            with them inside me. I fall asleep
            in that golden glow.

GINA   *(her voice husky with desire)* Good
            God, you certainly have a golden
            tongue.

ALBERTO   I'm glad you remember.

*(ALBERTO flickers his tongue suggestively, then
scoops GINA up in his arms and carries her to the
bedroom.)*

SCENE 6

*Looking suspicious, Pancho VILLA comes into the
living room. Over his shoulder he wears
ammununition straps and his pistol. A woman in*

29

turn of the century dress enters, carrying a tray
with a tea service.

WOMAN   Sit down, my General. Make
         yourself at home.

VILLA   (looking around) Don't worry, I
         will.

(The woman kneels to put the tray down on the
coffee table. Villa goes and sits down in front of
her.)

WOMAN   Let me pour you some tea. It's
         linden tea. Or would you rather
         have coffee?

VILLA   Hmmmmmn, I'd prefer coffee.

WOMAN   Linden tea is soothing, my
         General. It makes you think
         pleasant thoughts. It's very good
         for the nerves.

Lights up on the bedroom. GINA and ALBERTO
                are under the sheets, sitting up
                against the headboard and looking at
                the ceiling.

VILLA   That is exactly why I never touch
               it. I don't want my nerves to go
               all limp on me. Then you'd never
               get me out of your house.

WOMAN   Oh General, now who wants you
               to leave?

VILLA   You're extremely beautiful.

ALBERTO   She was a very beautiful woman.

VILLA   Very "well-bred", very "refined".
               From a "good family". You
               almost make me want to curl up
               at your feet.

GINA   Then the General drank the
               linden tea in a single gulp.

ALBERTO   No, he couldn't. He pretended to
               sip it. He never ate or drank
               anything that his sergeant hadn't
               tried and survived first. People
               had tried to poison Villa many
               times. He just pretended to sip it;

31

he was just buying a little more time.

GINA   Can you pass the jujubes.

ALBERTO   *(taking a jujube and passing the bag to her)* Yes, he was just buying a little more time.

GINA   Time for what?

ALBERTO   To enjoy the woman, to savour her slowly, and to say goodbye to her. Because that woman wasn't going to be <u>his</u>. At least not like all the other women the General had.

GINA   He had three hundred.

ALBERTO   No one really knows. The numbers are lost in the myth.

VILLA   You are like a desert flower.

ALBERTO   But she was very, I mean <u>very</u> beautiful.

VILLA   Yes, you are the loveliest flower I have ever seen. What rotten luck.

WOMAN   Drink your tea, my General.

GINA   And then you'll fall asleep in my arms.

WOMAN   And then you'll fall asleep in my arms.

VILLA   General Villa sleeps only in the arms of the desert and the open night. Son of a gun! You are like a rose in full bloom—but you're an enemy of the Revolution. Your father is one of Calles' generals.

GINA   So, what does it matter. She is who she is.

VILLA   Anyone can see that you always sleep on a white pillow. You're not even a tiny bit scared of me. You already imagine me waking up in your arms, don't you?

WOMAN   Let me pour you some more tea.
          Some more linden tea.

*(The woman holds out her arm to take his cup.
VILLA observes her. With the hand that isn't
holding the cup, he draws his pistol. He kills the
WOMAN. GINA's mouth hangs open. VILLA
blows the gunpowder off his pistol. ALBERTO gets
out of bed while VILLA gets off the sofa. As
ALBERTO talks to GINA, he gets dressed. His
movements strangely synchronized with
ALBERTO'S, VILLA removes the WOMAN's
earrings and closes her eyes. Then VILLA puts on
his boots and ammunition straps, preparing to
leave.)*

GINA   What the—! What happened?
          Why did he shoot her?

ALBERTO   Because I have to go.

GINA   Why?

ALBERTO   Because I have to go.

GINA   Stay and spend the night.

ALBERTO   I have to go.

34

GINA	We'll have supper and then you'll leave. The revolution isn't going to happen tonight.
VILLA	How does she know?
ALBERTO	How do you know?
GINA	You can do some work here.
ALBERTO	I didn't bring any.
GINA	Well bring some next time. I'm not asking you to spend the night, just to stay a bit longer. Alberto, at least stay for supper.
ALBERTO	I can't, I can't. I can't.
GINA	Then bring over the latest chapters and I'll type them up for you.
ALBERTO	Okay. Now I have to go.

VILLA puts on his spurs, tightens his belt, puts on his hat, while

ALBERTO puts on his shoes, opens and looks
through his wallet and
closes it, and runs his hand through his hair.

GINA   Fuck. You're always leaving.

VILLA   Attacking or running away.
            That's a man's lot, señorita.

VILLA and ALBERTO start when they hear the
doorbell. Startled, both men sneak away: VILLA
offstage, ALBERTO into the living room.

SCENE 7

GINA puts on a silk dressing gown and goes to
open the door. ISAAC is there.

GINA   Oh—Isaac, how are you? Come
            in, come in. Alberto, this is Isaac.
            He's a friend of my son's.

ALBERTO   Nice to meet you.

GINA   He works with me in the store.
            He designs blocks for me.

ALBERTO   How interesting.

GINA   <u>You</u> know, those little wooden
            toys for children.

ALBERTO   Of course.

GINA   He's designing the blocks for the
            maquiladora.

ALBERTO   You don't say. You're a block
            designer. That's very nice.

GINA   And this is Alberto Pineda, my,
            uh, my—

ISAAC   (*Coughs*) Pleased to meet you.

GINA   —good friend Alberto Pineda.

ISAAC   Oh, I've read your editorials.

ALBERTO   What a charming earring.

GINA   Show us the new blocks, Isaac.
            You'll see what beautiful work
            this boy does. He's even designed
            a special anti-gravity block that
            floats in the air.

ALBERTO   I'll be in touch, all right?

GINA   Wait a moment.

ALBERTO   No.

GINA   Just one moment.

ALBERTO   (*He folds his arms and waits exactly
            one moment.*) I'll be in touch. (*He
            kisses her and leaves.*)

*Brusquely, GINA closes the door behind him. As
she turns around, she bumps into ALBERTO'S
suitcase. She opens the door as he rings the bell,
kicks the suitcase outside and slams the door. She
grows sad. Slowly, emotionally, she pours herself a
tequila at the living room bar. She kicks the cassette
player to turn it on. (This is how Gina's tape
machine works) A romantic bolero plays.
GINA slumps onto the sofa. There, in her silk
dressing gown, her hair loose, she is languid and
spaced out. ISAAC has been watching her for the
last few moments, rapt. After a while GINA sighs
deeply, ISAAC coughs. GINA turns around,
surprised to see him.*

GINA   (*Languid, melancholy,
            melodramatic*) Isaac.

ISAAC   Yeah?

GINA   Isaac, come over here...

ISAAC   Yes?

GINA   ...show me your little blocks.

ISAAC   Sure.

ISAAC kneels beside the coffee table and starts taking out his blocks.

Slow blackout.

ACT TWO

SCENE 1

It is dark. GINA, in her silk dressing gown with a shawl over her shoulders, is sitting at a computer consulting one of Alberto's notebooks. Nearby are an empty glass and a half-empty bottle of tequila.

GINA   *(Typing)* It was a warm, clear night. *(Night comes up on the cyclorama.)* A crescent moon hung in the inky sky like a gleaming sickle. *(A crescent moon appears.)*

As GINA pours herself some tequila, then resumes typing, VILLA enters and holds his hands out towards her.

VILLA   Mamacita.

Gina continues typing.

VILLA   Mamacita!

Gina looks up, gasps, then giggles. She rises, walks over to Villa, holding Alberto's manuscript, and wraps her shawl around her rebozo-style.
N.B. In this scene Villa jumps over there sofa several times as though he were jumping over barricades.

VILLA   *(handing Gina a pouch)* Mamacita.

GINA withdraws items from the pouch, examines them, and throws them to the ground. She speaks in the same Hollywood Mexican accent as Villa does.

GINA   Some pieces of yellow
                glass.

VILLA   *(Catching the jewels or
                picking the up from the
                        ground)* They're <u>topaz</u>.

GINA   A ring with a brown
                stone—

VILLA   That stone is a tiger eye. Look,
                mamacita, these earrings are
                rubies.

GINA   I don't want these things, my son.
          In eighteen years I seen you only
          five times.

VILLA   Seven, mamacita.

GINA   Five.

VILLA   Seven.

GINA   Five, carajo!

VILLA   All right, mamacita, seven—I
          mean five.

GINA   And then you bring me jewels.

VILLA   Don't you like them, mamacita?

GINA   What do you want me to do with
          riches like these? Wear them to
          stroll around the town square, so
          that everyone can see and know
          that my son is a bandido?

VILLA   A revolutionary, mamacita.

GINA   The only time you come to see
         me is when one of your wars is in
         the area—or when you're
         committing some crime nearby.

VILLA   Ay, mamacita, you're starting to
         nag me already.

GINA   Look at this earring. Look—
         there's a drop of blood on it. And
         here—take your gold away once
         and for all, Pancho. Your mother
         is a poor woman, but at least she
         has dignity. *(She throws the
         jewellery at his feet.)*

VILLA   *(mariachi shriek)*
         Ayayayayay, mamacita, you sure
         have cojones!

GINA   You <u>need</u> cojones to be a mother.
         (shift in tone) Pancho, look how
         you live, always running for your
         life. Who darns your socks? Who
         makes sure your serape is clean?
         And if you have a toothache, who
         do you tell?

VILLA	There are lots of women out there who love me—
GINA	But not <u>one</u> of them married to you by the Church and in the eyes of God.
VILLA	What do you mean? <u>Five</u> of them married to me by the Church and in the eyes of God.
GINA	*(crossing herself)* Jesús Santo! *(Gina suddenly returns to her own voice)* I want names!
VILLA	What did you say, mamacita?
GINA	*(returning to the keyboard and typing)* You're going to give me names and addresses of all five of them, PLUS all your girlfriends. The old ones AND the ones you have now.
VILLA	What did you say, mamacita?
GINA	Oops, sorry. What am I doing? I'm sorry. *(She backspaces*

frantically and starts correcting:
Then, both Gina and Villa
"rewind" through their steps until
they are face to face again. GINA
resumes the accent.)

GINA   Jesús Santo! *(She crosses herself.)*
            What a disaster! That's as good as
            having no wife at all. Because if
            you have five, it means there's no
            one keeping an eye on you, my
            son. There's noone taking care of
            you night after night. Noone
            whose arms you know you'll die
            in...

(GINA sobs.)

VILLA   Don't cry, mamacita, or I'll go to
            pieces.

And VILLA goes to pieces. He cries. He takes the
bottle of tequila from Gina's little table and drinks.
GINA takes the bottle away from VILLA and drinks
too, also crying.

GINA   *(wiping away her tears)* And how
            many grandchildren do I have?

VILLA   A lot.

GINA   How many?

VILLA   You mean exactly? Well, there must be a hundred... A hundred and... I'm really sorry but I don't know the exact number. Anyway, we're forging a nation.
He kneels in front of her.
Don't get angry with me, mamacita. You know that I'm walking these roads of dust and blood so that your little grandchildren, mamacita, will have dignity like you, but also food in their bellies. <u>And</u> know how to read and write.

GINA   And how long are you going to go on like this, making war?

VILLA   Until we hang all the enemies of the Revolution from the belltowers of the Cathedral. *(The doorbell rings.)* Especially that general Elías Calles—we'll string him up by his cojones. *(The doorbell rings again.)*

GINA   And then?

VILLA   Until we make the world the way it should be.

GINA *(Crying)* Good luck... *(The doorbell rings again.)*
         Stop jumping all over the place.

VILLA   It's just that I don't like going around things. Give me your blessing, mamacita, I have to go now.
         (He kneels.)

GINA   I'm not giving you anything. First you're going to the priest to confess, then we'll see.

VILLA   I'm begging you, mamacita. When I was a child you hardly had any food to give me. I only ask you for a blessing...

The front door opens, and
PAULINA and ISAAC enter.
ISAAC is carrying a florist's box.
Villa waits, frozen on his knees, his
head bowed.

PAULINA   *(to Isaac)* Good thing I have a key.
            (calling) Gina?

GINA   I'm not giving you anything at
            all.

PAULINA: *(seeing GINA)* Gina?

GINA   *(in her own voice)* Oh.

PAULINA   We're supposed to go over the
            accounts tonight?

GINA: Uh, just a minute.

VILLA   *(becoming animated again)* Look,
            mamacita, if I go to confession I
            need at least eight days and you
            can hear for yourself the war is
            waiting for me out   there. And
            besides, you'd have to get me a
            priest with a very big heart,

48

bigger than my own, so I   could
tell him everything God gives me
license to do.

GINA   (*reading aloud from the notebook
            sans accent as she performs the
            action*) "The old woman's
            trembling hand glided over her
            son's head... but she pulled it
            away, as though she had touched
            fire." (*to Villa, resuming accent*) No,
            my son. I cannot give my blessing
            to a murderer.

VILLA   It does not matter, I'm used to it.
            Time to go.

(*VILLA exits. In the distance we see him fire into
the air three times. GINA drinks a gulp of tequila.*)

SCENE 2

PAULINA   This is outrageous, absolutely
            outrageous. He wants to hang my
            grandfather from his private
            parts in the middle of the main
            square. I don't know what his

problem is. Well, it's typical—
typical for a historian to be living
in the past.

GINA   You're taking it awfully
personally.

ISAAC places a vase of roses in the
living room, then withdraws. There's
a bolt of lightning outside.

PAULINA   There's going to be a storm... No,
why would I take it personally? If
I could, I'd do what my
grandfather did with the most
critical and most influential
intellectuals of his time: send
them off to Czechoslovakia—as
"ambassadors". It taught them to
keep their ideas "in check." *(GINA*
pours herself another tequila) Why
don't you stop, huh? You've
already had three quarters of a
bottle.

GINA   It was only up to here when I
started. OK, you don't see eye to

eye with him politically. I can
accept that. But as a writer —

PAULINA   As a writer, what really
impresses me is his —

GINA   Style.

PAULINA   No, no, his handwriting. His
periods and commas are really
something. They're so virile,
don't you think?

(Another lightning bolt.)

GINA   What are these roses?

PAULINA   They're from...*(she nods towards
ISAAC who is standing at the
window with his back to them)*

ISAAC turns around.

ISAAC   I mean, it's obvious: You have to
ask him to live with you.

GINA   What are you talking about? I'm very happy and serene living alone.

ISAAC   I'm talking about your insomnia, the days you don't come in to work—about the fact that the only thing you've being doing lately is typing that's guy's stuff; I'm talking about the fact that you've been drinking like a— *(there is a clap of thunder)* I don't understand. If two people, I mean, love each other, well—

PAULINA   It's a pact between adults, Isaac. They see each other, they enjoy each other, they have their own lives and that's it. Let's go over the notes for the maquiladora.

ISAAC   Gina, you should go and—I mean—confront him. Tell him: what I want most in the world is...to live with you.

(Another lightning bolt. GINA sobs.)

ISAAC   Gina, you have to give him an ultimatum. You have to tell him "It's all or nothing."

PAULINA   Let's not talk about him anymore, it's painful for her.

GINA   No, no, go on. Even if it hurts, keep talking about him.

ISAAC   If I were him, and you came to my place and, I don't know, and said to me—

GINA AND PAULINA   That's out of the question.

PAULINA   Gina can't go to his apartment.

ISAAC   Why not?

GINA   The pact. I'm not the kind of woman who goes behind a man's back. Who chases them and invades their privacy and... I'm not that kind of woman. What would you do if you were at home working on your blocks,

53

and I showed up at midnight and suddenly asked you to marry me?

PAULINA   *(Admonishing)* To marry you?

GINA   If I arrived with these red roses here... and said to you: Isaac, let's make a baby.

ISAAC   Those—? I... I'd uh...uh...

PAULINA   Gina, you already have a baby, and his Harvard tuition is costing you a fortune.

ISAAC   I'd love to make a baby with you. I'd be thrilled by your proposition. How could I deny you anything, impose constraints on you, forbid anything—I mean—if I loved you. Love aspires to be eternal, otherwise, it isn't love. *(A beat, during which PAULINA and GINA stare at ISAAC.)* If it isn't eternal, it's an unworthy love. And besides... *(ISAAC shuts up.)*

54

GINA   *(To Paulina)* That boy's worth
            keeping around.

PAULINA   Totally. What a surprise, Isaac.
            You're quite the philosopher.
            Let's hear the rest. Come on.

GINA   Yes, go on. Don't be shy.

PAULINA   You'd better not keep it in. Spit it
            out.

ISAAC   Deep down, what all men want is
            someone to turn everything
            upside down, who'll break
            through everything, all our
            idiotic defenses, someone to
            conquer us, to make us hers, to
            free us from ourselves. Well,
            that's my experience.

PAULINA   Yes, but you don't have any
            experience, Isaac.

*(GINA stands up and goes to the coatstand where
she takes off her dressing gown and puts on her
raincoat and high-heeled shoes.)*

55

PAULINA   What are you doing?

GINA   I'm going to break down his idiotic defenses.

PAULINA   Right now? Wait.

GINA   I'm going to his apartment.

PAULINA   We have a meeting tonight! At least call him first. Tell him you're coming over.

ISAAC   No, she has to catch him off guard.

PAULINA   Gina, what if he's annoyed that you've come over without telling him first. What if he gets mad. What if he's with... what if he gets mad.

(GINA stops, paralyzed)

ISAAC   What is there to get mad about? He's a left-wing radical, he'll understand. Anyway, if he gets mad, then Gina will throw the

roses in his face and say goodbye
to him forever. And she'll leave.
Like a lady.

GINA   I like that. I'll say goodbye to him
            forever and I'll leave *(with a
            theatrical gesture)* like a Queen...
            and then... I'll kill myself.

PAULINA   Fine, but do it tomorrow. *(GINA
            takes the flowers out of the vase.)* Do
            it tomorrow. *(GINA looks at the
            front door.)* At least put some
            clothes on.

GINA   What for, if he's just going to take
            them off. *(GINA starts to walk
            towards the door, looking somewhere
            between regal and insecure. She
            stumbles backwards three steps, then
            starts walking forward again.)* I'll
            take a taxi. *(A lightning bolt
            illuminates her exit.)*

Blackout

PAULINA   Shit. The power's out.

ISAAC   She's got to have candles around
here somewhere.

SCENE 3

*The front door of Alberto's
apartment building. It is raining.
GINA presses a buzzer.*

VOICE ON THE INTERCOM   Who is it?

GINA   Me. *(Silence.)* Do you hear me, Alberto?
It's me. Alberto...? Don't you hear me? It
isn't buzzing. *(She pushes on the door, to
no avail.)* Alberto? Alberto, it isn't
buzzing to let me in. *(The door opens.
ALBERTO comes out and closes it behind
him. GINA's tone becomes passionate)*
Alberto, let's make a baby.

*ALBERTO opens an umbrella. GINA tries to understand
what this means.*

GINA   Aren't you going to invite me up?

Silence. We hear the rain falling.

ALBERTO   I can't. There's... There's...
upstairs—another, oh God.
Another woman.

GINA   Marta.

ALBERTO   What?

GINA   Marta, your wife.

ALBERTO   No, no. Are you crazy?

GINA   Then the other one, your first
wife. What's her name?

ALBERTO   Who?

GINA   Your first wife?

ALBERTO   No. No. No.

GINA   Who, then?

ALBERTO   It doesn't matter. I swear, it
doesn't matter.

GINA   Tell me.

ALBERTO   She doesn't have a name, she
           doesn't exist.

GINA   *(under her breath)*...in his face and
           say goodbye...

ALBERTO   What?

GINA   ...forever. Do you hear me? It's
           over for good.

(She tries to hit him with the roses but he dodges the blow. GINA falls to the ground.)

GINA   *(Standing up)* Shit: my heel.
           *(ALBERTO bends down to pick up
           the heel that has come off her shoe.)*
           Hold still, you bastard.

ALBERTO   Your face, Gina... Your face is
           hurt. *(GINA touches her face: there
           are five drops of blood.)* No, it's
           from your fingers, you pricked
           them...

GINA   It's only blood, Alberto. Now
           hold still, you bastard.

*ALBERTO obeys, and stands still under the
umbrella while GINA backs up a few steps and
takes aim. She throws the roses in his face, turns
around and starts to walk away, limping, in the
rain. She is illuminated by a bolt of lightning.*

SCENE 4

*The apartment. PAULINA and ISAAC sit by
candlelight. ISAAC looks at his watch. PAULINA
looks at her watch.*

PAULINA   Well, she stayed to sleep with
            him. Let's go.

ISAAC   She could have called to let us
            know.

PAULINA   She was blinded by passion.

ISAAC   She still could have called. How long
            does a phonecall take? One minute.
            *(PAULINA observes him slyly, but
            touched at the same time.)* Maybe we
            should call the hospitals.

PAULINA   We'll see tomorrow.

ISAAC   I'm not leaving till she gets home.

PAULINA   There are blankets in the closet.

ISAAC   Yeah.

PAULINA   I'll take a candle.

ISAAC   No, I'm calling the police.

PAULINA   Nighty night.

            *PAULINA blows him a kiss. She
            leaves.*
            *ISAAC goes into the kitchen. We
            hear him talking on the phone.*

ISAAC   (pause) Hello? I'd like to report a
            missing person. Yes, thank you.
            (pause) Hello? I'd like to report a
            missing person. Yes, thank you.
            Hello? I'd like to report—oh yes.
            Gina Benítez. Three days—I
            mean three hours.

SCENE 5

The door opens in the dark. GINA enters without closing the door behind her. She bumps into a piece of furniture, making a racket. The lights come back on. ISAAC comes out of the kitchen holding the phone.

GINA   Shit.

(GINA is soaked to the skin, her makeup has run, her hair is a mess. A beat.)

GINA   What are you looking at?

ISAAC   What happened to you?

GINA   Nothing. "Life" happened to me. I went walking in the rain. Is that bad, according to your experience? I didn't kill myself, I'm here, now you can go.

ISAAC   Why don't you take a hot bath and go to bed?

GINA   *(Grabs the phone from him and drops into an armchair. She dials.)*

José, José, my baby. Your mother. Who do you think? I know it's three in the morning there, but it's two in the morning here, which is almost as— Who's there with you? I hear a voice. Margaret who? Delaware. And what are you two doing? Ah, trigonometry. So you and Margaret Delaware are going to spend the rest of the night studying trigonometry. Why are you lying to me, José? Why do all men lie? Your father, may he rest in peace, never lied to me. *(She looks at the receiver: José has hung up. She hangs up. She is very still.)* At least I don't think he did.

(ISAAC comes over and gives her a glass of cognac)

GINA   Haven't you left yet? *(She gets up and kicks the tape player to turn it on)*

ISAAC   I'll have to fix that thing.

GINA   No. That's just the way it is.

A bolero plays. GINA, suffused by the heartbreaking
words of the song, suffers along with the singer.
Until she becomes aware of Isaac, who has been
watching her. First, GINA is distressed. Then she
looks at ISAAC again, examining him thoroughly.
She removes her raincoat without taking her eyes off
him. ISAAC tenses up. Then he downs the cognac
in a single gulp and goes over to her. They dance
slowly, tenderly—and clumsily. ISAAC doesn't
know how to dance a bolero.)

GINA   You don't know how to lead.

ISAAC   So? You lead.

            They continue dancing. Their bodies
            gradually relax, and an intimacy
            begins to grow between them.

SCENE 6

ALBERTO enters in the dark, through the door that
GINA left open. He is holding a red rose. He
approaches. He stands looking at the dancing pair.
When GINA finally sees him, she continues
dancing.

ALBERTO   Leave us alone, Abraham.

ISAAC seeks GINA's eyes. GINA looks away.

ALBERTO   Leave us, Abraham.

ISAAC goes towards the front door, while ALBERTO goes over to GINA. The song ends and other one begins. ALBERTO pulls GINA close to dance; she doesn't react at first but then puts her arms around him too. They dance. ISAAC, after spying for a few moments, leaves noiselessly.

ALBERTO and GINA dance marvelously well and for a moment of fantasy even look like Fred Astaire and Ginger Rogers. They dance towards the bedroom. But at the doorway, ALBERTO presses GINA against the wall, pins her arms up over her head, undoes his fly and lifts one of her legs so that he can penetrate her. A furious struggle ensues. GINA breaks away from ALBERTO, runs to the tape player and turns it off with a kick.

ALBERTO   Fine. What do you want? What
           exactly is it that you want?

GINA   I want—I want to sleep with you
           every night. I want to wake up

with you every morning. I want
to have breakfast with you. I
want you to come and eat here
every day. I want to go on
vacation with you. I want a house
in the country. I want you to talk
to my son long distance, I want
the two of you to talk about men
things, and for me to bring you a
cup of tea while you're having a
serious conversation with my
son. I want you to end things
with Marta—I mean, officially, by
signing divorce papers. I want a
gold necklace with my name on
it. I want to discipline myself
once and for all to go running
every morning. I want to quit
smoking. I want you to come
with me to Juarez to choose the
land for the maquiladora. I want
a house by the sea. And I want... I
want to wake up with you. Open
my eyes every morning and see
you. I want to see you and close
my eyes and go to sleep in peace.
And I want you, twenty years

from now, to hold me.... and tell me: "life is good.

ALBERTO   And you wanted us to make a baby.

GINA   Go figure.

ALBERTO   All right.

GINA   And I want to remember everything that I want and not just care about what you or José or Paulina or everyone else wants.

ALBERTO   All right. Take out your diaphragm.

GINA   What?

ALBERTO   If you want us to make a baby.

GINA   Yeah, sure, that's the easy part. But everything else I'm asking for you don't want.

ALBERTO   I said, all right. All right. All
          right. All right. *(ALBERTO draws*
          close.) I want... a life with you.
          <u>That</u> I know. Life with you is
          good. *(He kisses her slowly. They*
          caress each other. It'll be a baby girl
          with big round eyes.

SLOW BLACKOUT as the caresses continue.

ACT THREE

SCENE 1

The apartment. Late afternoon. During the scene, the light will almost imperceptibly grow red. GINA opens the door. ALBERTO is there, his shoulder against the doorframe, a cigarette in his mouth. He's about to say something, but coughs instead.

GINA Do you have a cold?

ALBERTO   A bit of one.

GINA   Then you shouldn't be smoking. Since when do you smoke?

ALBERTO   Since last week. *(He looks for a place to put out the cigarette.)*

GINA Over there.

ALBERTO   What?

GINA   In the plant. *(He butts the cigarette out in the plant and starts to take off his coat.)* No, wait. Don't.

ALBERTO   Why not?

GINA   We'll go have coffee somewhere.

ALBERTO   *(Thinks about this. Walks toward the sofa. Sits down.)* I know I haven't called for three months. *(A long beat.)* That's a long time. But—I don't know if you can understand me—it's also a very short time. I know you have a full life without me, so you don't <u>need</u> me. And I don't need you. What you and I have is something unique. It's a gift—something precious that life has given us. What we have belongs to another realm. A realm that exists a centimetre—a minute—outside of this world, outside of time. In one sense, three months is a lot. And yet in another, it's nothing. Because yesterday—it was hardly yesterday—I went out that door. Barely yesterday I went out of your body. *(GINA remains standing.)* I had work: the university, two or three challenging editorials; I revised the manuscript and gave it to the publisher. *(ALBERTO waits for some kind of reaction from GINA. In vain.)* My book on Villa—I gave it to the publisher. *(No reaction from GINA.)* And I went down the Yucatan, to cover the electoral fraud and... Anyway.

GINA   Three months. Thirteen weeks. Ninety-one days. Never mind the days. Ninety-two nights.

(A beat)

ALBERTO   The way you're leaning against that column over there, in the reddish light from the sunset, you look like a... *(GINA abruptly goes and sits on one of the sofas)* ...like a Greek Goddess.

GINA   Three months ago you called and said you were on your way over. The night before, we had decided A LOT OF THINGS. You said it was important for us to talk—what

did you say—urgent. No,
CRUCIAL, that was the word you
used. I waited all afternoon.
That's a lie. I waited for you until
dawn.

ALBERTO   What happened is—you're not
            going to believe me.

GINA You're probably right.

ALBERTO   Something incredible happened. I
            was on my way over here. I was
            stuck on the freeway. You know
            where the train tracks run almost
            parallel to the freeway? Well,
            traffic was bumper to bumper—
            we were barely moving, and
            there I was with that huge
            erection that always happens—
            that huge erection that just
            <u>happens</u> to me whenever I'm
            coming to see you. Then I
            glanced toward the tracks. There
            was a campesino with a straw
            hat, walking beside them. And
            then a train—a train came
            speeding by and suddenly I saw

the campesino's head fly up in the air. It happened in a split second: the head flew up and while the train was going by I couldn't see him anymore. I was gripping the steering wheel as though I'd seen the Devil himself. When the train had passed, the campesino was nowhere in sight. I thought I'd ben hallucinating. Everything went out of my mind—even where I was going. I tried to get off the freeway, to get to the train tracks, to see if the head—or the body—was there. I never got there. I got off the freeway and got lost in some slum. *(A beat.)* That's what happened.

GINA   And the next ninety days?

ALBERTO   Well... I swear to you, I don't know. I took what happened on the freeway as a bad omen. I was in shock. You know how superstitious I am.

GINA   News to me.

ALBERTO   Well, it turns out I am. I started to
            work like a fiend for the next few
            days, the next few weeks... I don't
            know, it felt like I was going to
            die. I had this strange certainty I
            was going to die—but first, I had
            to finish the book. I finished it
            and I took it to the publisher. *(He
            waits for a reaction from GINA. In
            vain.)* But honestly, I don't know,
            I don't know what happened out
            there. By the way, <u>you</u> could
            have phoned me.

GINA   According to our pact—

ALBERTO   You could have broken the pact.

GINA   I broke it once and I regretted it.

A beat.

ALBERTO   It's really strange: when I think
            about you, I think of your hands,
            of your mouth, your breasts, your
            legs... some part of your body. It's

75

not until I see you again that
everything comes together in a
specific person, a living,
breathing, thinking person... That
terrifies me—knowing you exist
without me.

*GINA bursts into tears, but to hide them, runs into
the bedroom.*

GINA   *(as she leaves)* Don't come after
            me. *(She closes the door behind her.)*

ALBERTO   Oh, you're going to make tea?
            No, I guess not.

*ALBERTO sits on the sofa. There's something hard
under the cushion. He looks under the seat and
finds a wooden block and a wooden heart. He looks
at the wooden heart.*

ALBERTO   How goddamned childish.

*Hearing GINA returning, he quickly shoves the
block and wooden heart back under the cushion and
feigns calm.)*

GINA   Alberto, look—

ALBERTO   About our baby.

GINA   No. It was a crazy idea.

ALBERTO   Not at all. Why? I talked to my
wife—to Marta.

GINA   I know what her name is.

ALBERTO   She said she didn't have a
problem. She said we could have
a baby.

GINA   (*overwhelmed*) She didn't have a
problem—with a baby I would be
having. I don't imagine she
would. I didn't know you were so
intimate with Marta—I mean,
still.

ALBERTO   We're friends, that's all. I'm
telling you what I told her so
you'd know my intentions were
serious. Are serious. At least
about the baby. As for the rest,
that's what I wanted to discuss.I
wanted to talk it over with you

point by point. The house by the
sea is fine, but—

GINA   Alberto, listen to me.

ALBERTO   Sit down.

GINA   I don't want to.

ALBERTO   All right, stand up, it's your
            house.

GINA   Alberto, no more... it's all over.
            Don't come here anymore, I don't
            even want you to phone me.

ALBERTO   You mean... it's over?

GINA   It's all over. OVER.

ALBERTO   (hysterical) That's just great, it's all
            over. Fine: it's all over. Perfect.
            it's all over. It was a pleasure
            knowing you. It's all over, it's all
            over. Time to go!

ALBERTO, worked up because "it's all over",
opens the door to leave. There, PANCHO VILLA is
waiting for him.

VILLA   Easy, compañero Pineda, easy,
cálmate. With a rose petal. Like
the wind that caresses the valleys
and lifts skirts.

ALBERTO   *(going back to Gina)* I'm sorry I
disappeared for three months,
but... we can work everything
out.

GINA   No.

ALBERTO   Everything. *(He touches her.)*

GINA   No!

VILLA   Even if it does not look like it,
she's giving in. Just play her
strings softly—any minute now
she'll start to sing.

ALBERTO touches GINA again. She moves far
away.

ALBERTO   What the hell's happened to you.
          You've always said yes to
          everything; now suddenly today
          it's no, no and no. I can't come to
          your home. You don't want to
          have my baby. You won't let me
          touch you. I can't even give you a
          compliment. Open up,
          goddamit!

GINA   I'm in love.

A long beat.

VILLA   Ingrate. *(He turns around. He has a
          knife in his back.)*

ALBERTO   Chief!

VILLA   It's nothing, just a fucking knife.
          Go on. *(He starts trying to pull out
          the knife.)*

ALBERTO   Excuse me, I think I heard you
          wrong. You're what?

GINA   In love.

ALBERTO   Oh please. Language like that at
            your age. In love! Would you
            care to elaborate?

GINA   No. It's very simple. I'm in love.

ALBERTO   It's hardly "simple". There's an
            extensive bibliography on that
            delusional state. From Plato to
            Freud, to Kierkegaard, Marcuse
            and the post-Freudians. "In love".
            You might be sexually aroused.
            *(VILLA manages to get the knife out
            of his back. ALBERTO continues,
            more sure of himself)* Perhaps you
            feel a certain sexual curiosity
            towards someone. In love. You're
            just trying to hurt me. I'm still
            waiting for a functional definition
            of the term.

GINA   ...

ALBERTO   With who?

GINA   ...

VILLA   Let's see if they show their faces,
               the little sons of bitches.

ALBERTO   With that jerk with the earring—I
               don't know why I'm even asking.
               That wimpy little faggot.
               Ezekiel?

GINA   Isaac.

A bang. VILLA jumps and turns around. He has a
bullet wound in his forearm.

VILLA   Fuck. And me with only my soul
to protect me...

VILLA takes off his bandana to bandage his forearm.
He keeps looking around, paranoid.

ALBERTO   Fine, we'll analyze the situation
               calmly and coolly, all right? I'm
               gone for three months and you
               replace me with a kid your son's
               age.

GINA   Older.

ALBERTO   One year older. Are you going to
            support him?

GINA   No. Why?

VILLA starts loading his pistol.

ALBERTO   Is he going to pay your son's
            tuition?

GINA   We each take care of our own
            expenses. Anyway, you'd be
            surprised to know how much he
            earns. More than you do.

ALBERTO   Ah yes, his boss pays him well.

GINA   It has nothing to do with money.

ALBERTO   Are you going to give him a
            raise? Or are you going to make
            him a partner right away?

GINA   We each take care of our own
            expenses, didn't you hear me?

ALBERTO   Of course, it's not like you're
            going to get married.

GINA smiles.

VILLA   I need water, a sip of water. *(He goes to the kitchen)* You keep it up, compañero.

ALBERTO   And what does this have to do with us? I told you: Our relationship is beautiful because it's outside the mainstream of everyday life. Of life and death. What we have belongs to another realm. It's you and me. Me and you. I don't care about him. Listen: if you love him, I... I accept it.

VILLA returning from the kitchen, is hit by another bullet.

VILLA   What the hell...? Now there is shooting from our own ranks.

ALBERTO   I can't make any demands on her, Chief. She's a thinking woman.

VILLA   What's that?

ALBERTO   She earns her own living. I don't have any leverage. How can I convince her?

VILLA   What do you mean how? *(He pats his crotch)* With feelings.

ALBERTO   I'm trying, but—

VILLA   There's no way in hell you share your woman! You sure don't share your gun or your horse!

ALBERTO   That's why you lost power, Chief, 'cause you were so too stubborn to negotiate.

VILLA   You are wrong, amigo. With bourgeois traitors like that you don't negotiate, you make demands—you shoot. Because as soon as you open the door, they want to move right in.

GINA   It's better for me to tell you right away.

VILLA   Here it comes.

ALBERTO   What else?

VILLA   Don't let her talk, for fuck's sake!
Hit her, kiss her, tell her how cute
she is when she is angry.

ALBERTO   You're so cute when—

GINA   We're going to live together.

VILLA gets hit by another bullet.

ALBERTO   *(wide-eyed)* To live together...
here?

GINA   Yes.

ALBERTO   I mean... All right. All right, we'll
find—

VILLA   All right? All right? You wimp!
I'm out of here.

*VILLA gets up, but because he's in pain from the
gunshot wounds, he walks slowly and laboriously
towards the door.*

GINA   We'll find what?

ALBERTO   (His attention is torn between GINA
           and VILLA who is leaving) We'll
           find another place to get together.
           I'm not jealous.

VILLA is hit by another bullet.

VILLA   Ayy.

GINA   (Emphatically) No.

Another bullet.

ALBERTO   Why not? I'm making it easy for
           you.

GINA   Because I'm in love up to my
           eyeballs.

Another gunshot. VILLA is knocked down. A beat.
VILLA stands up with difficulty, riddled with
bulletholes.

ALBERTO   Is he in there?

GINA   Who?

ALBERTO   In the bedroom, listening to
           everything.

GINA   Who?

ALBERTO   Come on out, kid, I know you're
           in there.

GINA   There's noone there.

*VILLA goes into the bedrooom. ALBERTO moves
towards the bedroom, but GINA blocks his way. He
pushes her aside and enters. VILLA drags out
ISAAC and beats him mercilessly. He opens the
front door and throws him out. ALBERTO comes
back into the living room.*

GINA   There's noone there, how could
           you think...?

VILLA   Is done.

ALBERTO   Thanks.

*ALBERTO walks around the living room,
straightening things up. GINA opens the front door
pointedly.*

GINA   Alberto... did you drive here?

ALBERTO   I'm parked right in front of the
              building, I'm going. Sit down. Sit
              down, I swear, I'm almost out the
              door. I just want to look at you
              one last time. Just a few
              moments—my last few moments
              with you—if that's all right.

*GINA closes the front door and rests her shoulder
against it.*

*ALBERTO sits down on the sofa. VILLA goes over
to GINA. A long silence.*

ALBERTO   I just want to look at you.

*The curtains, lit by the reddish light of dusk are
moved by the heavy breeze).*

ALBERTO   To look at you.

*Silence. All we hear is VILLA's breathing, heavy
              and threatening.*

VILLA   There she was, in the red glow of
              dusk...Another woman, always

the same woman. I was broken, I
was dying— that afternoon,
death was invading my body,
and the pain from the lead in my
body was mixed with the pain of
understanding: another woman,
always the same woman.

GINA (*Gradually becoming frightened*)
Don't do that.

ALBERTO Don't do what?

VILLA I am just looking at you.

ALBERTO Nothing's going to happen, I
swear.

VILLA I'm just seeing how the light
changes your face. You've always
been the same woman. No matter
how often I trade you for
another, you've always been the
same one, one and the same, one
single woman.

ALBERTO You know, in the light of the
sunset you look...especially...

VILLA   Green.

ALBERTO   Beautiful. Like a statue—

VILLA   Made of oxidized copper.

ALBERTO   Beautiful and—

VILLA   Green.

ALBERTO   And so...

VILLA   She's just another woman,
             compañero. You'll go and she'll
             stay standing beside this door
             forever, like a statue. She'll stay
             closed in her own little world and
             you'll find other welcoming
             arms—there's never any shortage
             of those. Younger arms. Softer
             ones. More innocent eyes.

ALBERTO   Gina... you're the last woman I'll
             ever love...

VILLA   Andale. We may be wounded but
             we're not dead yet.

ALBERTO   I'll never give myself to anyone like this again.

VILLA   Just wrap it up already and take me to a doctor.

GINA   Maybe if I'd expressed what I wanted—if I hadn't said yes to everything, like you said before...If I'd asked you for what I needed, bit by bit, instead of hitting you with it all at once late one night—and had given you the chance to say bit by bit yes or no... But... I was afraid of you.

ALBERTO   Afraid? Of me?

GINA   I've been afraid of every man I've ever loved. Of my father, of my brother. Of Felipe. Of you.

ALBERTO   But why?

GINA   *(She thinks hard.)* Because... I don't know—Because you're all bigger than me.

ALBERTO   Gina.

GINA   Now I finally trust a man, but
            unfortunately it isn't you.

VILLA   When will this agony end? Son of
            a—

GINA   Don't Alberto. Don't cry, Alberto.

VILLA is hit by another bullet.

VILLA   *(in agony)* What humiliation!

ALBERTO   My tears are tears of rage. *(He has
            trouble breathing.)* You can't do
            this to me. *(He is choking)* Not to
            me.

GINA   Please, Alberto. Please go now.

ALBERTO   You can't. You can't. I won't let
            you. You can't.

VILLA   Like that compañero, like that.

ALBERTO   And you can't because—

VILLA   Kill her already. Later you can make your speech.

ALBERTO   I'm not that kid who...

VILLA   Just do it.

VILLA puts his hand on his pistol. ALBERTO puts his hand in the pocket of his raincoat. ALBERTO takes out, like a revolver, his book. VILLA draws.

GINA   What's that? The book on Villa?

ALBERTO   ...

GINA   You didn't tell me it was out already. You said you gave it to the publisher but not that it was already out!*(VILLA collapses in an armchair. ALBERTO gives GINA the book.)* I'll read it very carefully.

ALBERTO   *(choking with rancour)* You already know what it says.

GINA   It doesn't matter. I'm going to read every word. That's great, huh, Villa on the cover, on horseback. *(Curious, VILLA comes over to look at his picture.)* And on the back cover, you at your desk. You look very intriguing. And very handsome. The typeface is perfect. Courrier 11 point. Very easy to read.

ALBERTO   It's courrier DELUXE.

ALBERTO moves away. He walks around, looking at the reddened curtains.)

GINA   I'm happy for you, Alberto.

VILLA   *(secretly to ALBERTO)* Now we'll get her.

ALBERTO   *(Whining)* I dedicated it to you.

GINA   *(very surprised)* The book? Are you serious?

VILLA   Don't be a sissy.

GINA   I never would have imagined...

ALBERTO   No, really? That day I didn't
           show up I was coming to propose
           to you. You never would have
           imagined that either, eh?

GINA   But Alberto...

ALBERTO   What?

GINA   It's just that you're STILL
           MARRIED, Alberto.

VILLA draws his pistol.

VILLA   So?

ALBERTO   I intended to straighten that out
           too. The truth is you never had
           faith in me.

GINA   Well... no, I guess not, I never did
           have faith in you. Honestly, I'd
           never have imagined that you'd
           dedicate your book to me and
           now... I don't know—what to
           think—or do... I didn't think I
           was that—<u>important</u> to you.

Moved, GINA sits down beside ALBERTO.
ALBERTO puts his arm around her shoulders.
VILLA hovers over them, enjoying the lovers'
reunion. GINA looks through the first few pages of
the book. She reads. Shakes her head.

GINA   Oh, by hand. You inscribed it by
              hand. "To a dear friend, as
              passionate about Pancho Villa as
              I am."

VILLA   Boy, you really <u>are</u> a jerk.

GINA   Alberto, now I really have to ask
              you to go.

ALBERTO   It's so irresponsible to let yourself
              be carried away by instinct. Ours
              was a beautiful relationship
              based on lust, but you had to let
              yourself get carried away by the
              female urge to nest. You had to
              turn our passion into a matter of
              shared bathrooms and baby
              bottles and dry cleaning bills.
              You had to trap me here in your
              home, you had to conduct
              yourself like a "woman".

GINA   That's why you have to leave
              now.

VILLA   That's why you have to kill her.
              With your own hands.

ALBERTO   All right, I'll get divorced. It was
              just a formality—I was just too
              lazy to deal with it.

GINA   I don't care anymore.

ALBERTO   That day I was coming to
              propose to you...

GINA   Alberto, will you please go.

VILLA   Alberto, will you please kill her?

ALBERTO looks around the apartment longingly.
He moves away from GINA and VILLA, walks
around nervously, oblivious.

GINA   Alberto.

VILLA   Alberto.

GINA   Alberto. What are you waiting
              for?

VILLA   Alberto, what are you waiting
              for?

A beat.

GINA   Would you leave? Alberto?

VILLA   Would you wring her neck,
              Alberto?

ALBERTO runs to a window and jumps out.
A long beat.
GINA runs to the window and closes it. She turns
around, her mouth hanging open, in surprise.

GINA But my apartment's on the ground floor!

VILLA collapses, dead at last, of shame.

SLOW BLACKOUT.

ACT 4

SCENE 1

Night. The electric lights in the apartment come up. There's a knock at the door. PAULINA comes out of the bedroom and snorts a bit of coke as she crosses the living room. She opens the door. ALBERTO is standing there, his shoulder against the doorframe. ALBERTO and PAULINA stare at each other. He's wearing an old, battered, felt hat, a sweater without a shirt underneath, and a three-day beard.

PAULINA   You look at her... staring into her eyes. Breathing deeply. You kiss her. She says: Wait, sit down, I'll make some tea.

ALBERTO   She told you everything. You must be Paulina.

PAULINA   Paulina Elías. Of course she did, Alberto. She's my best friend.

ALBERTO   Is she home?

PAULINA   No.

ALBERTO   She hasn't come back since I
           called?

PAULINA   Make yourself comfortable.

PAULINA goes into the kitchen.

           ALBERTO obeys, surprised by
           Paulina's authoritative tone. He
           hangs his raincoat on the coatrack.

ALBERTO   What time will she—

           He goes towards the window but
           retreats, dizzy with the memory of
           his failed suicide attempt.

ALBERTO   The ground floor. What time will
           she be back?

PAULINA comes back carrying a tray with a tea
service. She puts it down on the low coffee table and
kneels to serve it.

ALBERTO   What time—

PAULINA   She's out of town. She said if you
           called, not to tell you where she
           is.

ALBERTO   Why not?

PAULINA   Because a month ago, when she
           refused to let you in at two in the
           morning, you kicked in the front
           door of the building.

ALBERTO   You're very quick at making tea.

PAULINA   I put the water on when you said
           you were coming.

ALBERTO   I was drunk. I was desperate.
           And I had to talk to her. To
           somebody like her. Sombody
           understanding.

PAULINA   Two sugars?

ALBERTO   Someone who sees the glass as
           half full and not half empty. It's
           because that day I'd gone to
           Villa's funeral.

PAULINA   Two sugars?

ALBERTO   I mean, the <u>anniversary</u> of his
            funeral—I mean, the anniversary
            of his <u>death</u>. I went to the
            cemetary.

PAULINA is up to five spoonfuls of sugar.

ALBERTO   It tore my heart to shreds and I
            needed to see Gina. Is this linden
            tea?

PAULINA   No. It's rosehip. Is it good?

ALBERTO   *(sniffing it)* No. I don't drink tea.

PAULINA   So you went to the cemetery. Did
            anyone but <u>you</u> actually show
            up?

ALBERTO   Lots of people. About seven
            hundred, between Villa's children
            and grandchildren. It was
            enough to make you cry. They
            came from all over the country.
            There they were: dark-skinned
            and with the Centaur's eyes:

turquoise blue, clear and bright, like two drops of sky. Pure sky. There were a few widows too, very old now. And they just stood there—the children, the grandchildren, Villa's women— all looking at the grave. Humble folk. Lots of them illiterate. Half of them barefoot and the others in beat up old shoes. It really was enough to make you cry. What was the revolution for, what did General Pancho Villa fight for, if his grandchildren don't have any more hope than he did as a kid? The Revolution gave justice to others, the ones who <u>weren't</u> beside that grave. The educated ones. The ones with degrees. Those fucking bourgeois bastards.

PAULINA   Well, he had too many children, don't you think? He sowed children like they were ears of corn.

ALBERTO   What are you talking about? All
           his grandchildren worship his
           memory. It's the only thing that
           matters to them: the memory of
           the Centaur.

PAULINA   That's what I mean—the only
           thing he left them was his
           memory. No education, no jobs.
           Only his unattainable shadow.

ALBERTO   The enlightened oligarchy has
           spoken.

PAULINA   And then you got drunk.

ALBERTO   Villa's children broke my heart
           and yes, I went drinking, and I
           didn't drink a lot, but since I
           almost never drink, I got
           plastered, and then I needed to
           see Gina, I needed to talk to her.

PAULINA   About Villa.

ALBERTO   About Villa. Do you know the
           grave is empty?

PAULINA   Villa's grave?

ALBERTO   Actually, some people say that...
           in fact...

PAULINA   In fact what?

ALBERTO   Some people say that Villa
           jumped out of his grave all by
           himself.

PAULINA   Like Christ.

ALBERTO   Yep, like Christ he was
           resurrected and he rose out of the
           earth.

PAULINA   So you think he's alive
           somewhere?

ALBERTO   Saint Pancho Villa. Riding
           around on horseback. Well,
           anyway, he's around, isn't he,
           riding around in our
           imaginations at least. In our
           struggle for redemption. I don't
           know why I'm telling you all this.
           I mean, I don't even know you.

PAULINA   Don't worry, I enjoy listening to
          you. I'm mesmerized by your
          golden tongue. I liked your
          Pancho Villa book, too.

ALBERTO   Oh.

PAULINA   I bought it in the supermarket...
          and I read it in the check-out line.
          It's short.

ALBERTO   *(annoyed)* What time did you say
          she'd be back?

PAULINA   She's gone out of town. She's left
          the country.

ALBERTO   It's not true.

PAULINA   She sold me the apartment—
          everything included. Everything.

*ALBERTO walks around nervously. He stops in
front of a painting that wasn't there before. A
portrait in oils of former president Plutarco Elías
Calles, the tricoloured Mexican banner across his
chest.*

PAULINA   My grandfather. A bourgeois
          bastard.

ALBERTO   Uh huh. Where is she?

PAULINA   She asked me not to tell you.

ALBERTO   With that little jerk—Ishmael?

PAULINA   With Isaac, yes.

ALBERTO   Where?

PAULINA   I can't tell you.

ALBERTO   In Juarez, dealing with the
          maquiladora.

PAULINA doesn't answer.

ALBERTO   Well I'm going to go to Juarez
          and I'm going to comb the city.

PAULINA   Actually, she isn't in Juarez.
          Everything's under way there but
          Gina decided to take six months
          off from the business and she's—
          far away.

ALBERTO   Where?

PAULINA   I can't tell you.

ALBERTO   Why not?

PAULINA   I told you: because you kicked
           down the front door of the
           building.

ALBERTO   So what? I have the right to try
           and get her back. Paulina, I've
           changed. I don't know what she
           told you about me, but I've
           changed. I need her. Finally, in all
           humility, without any shame, I'm
           acknowledging that I need her. I
           need her.

PAULINA   ...

ALBERTO   You have to help me, Paulina. I'm
           a mess. I'm a wreck. I'm a basket
           case. I'm going bald.

PAULINA   Really!

ALBERTO   *(indicating his temples)* Two
          months ago I had alot more hair
          here.

PAULINA   Gee, that's terrible.

ALBERTO   My gums hurt. They bleed all the
          time. I went to the dentist and he
          said my problem was
          psychological. My body needs
          her. My soul does. This
          melancholy, this longing for a
          phantom, is eating away my
          brain. The other day I seriously
          thought about signing up for
          Transcendental Meditation. Can
          you see me turning myself into a
          mystic at my age, with my past of
          dialectical materialism?

PAULINA   And did you sign up?

ALBERTO   No. I didn't like the look of the
          guru. He was smiling too much,
          if you know what I mean.

PAULINA   No.

ALBERTO   I mean, coming from India, a
            country that's dying of hunger,
            and he's smiling... Smiling about
            what? The fact that India doesn't
            have milk but <u>does</u> have an atom
            bomb? I mean, they showed me a
            video of a guru smiling
            compulsively for forty-five
            minutes and what I did was beat
            the shit out of the instructor.

PAULINA   You hit the meditation teacher?

ALBERTO   I was in a bad mood. It doesn't
            matter. The fact is that—

PAULINA   It doesn't matter to you, but I'm
            sure the instructor—

*PAULINA cuffs ALBERTO on the side of the
            head..*

PAULINA   Take your punishment. *(She
            smiles.)*

ALBERTO   *(Raising his voice)* The fact is
            that... it's that...I've always
            carried the world on my

shoulders, and now I'm carrying my own destiny, and it's a heavier burden, because in addition to the weight of my destiny there's the knowledge that it doesn't matter in the least. You don't understand me.

PAULINA   I understand you perfectly.

ALBERTO   Not one bit.

PAULINA   You're saying that you feel weighed down by the mediocrity of your life.

ALBERTO   *(He walks around, annoyed by Paulina's interpretation.)* Not exactly. *(He goes and sits beside PAULINA.)* Paulina, let's be reasonable. You know it can't possibly work out with that kid.

PAULINA   Look, Alberto, I'm not saying for a moment that Isaac is any better than you. From what I know of you both, he isn't in a number of ways. You're more mature—at least physically; you're better read, although who knows what use that is. You're a better lover— as a lover you're better "equipped"—from what I hear. Oh, don't be embarrassed. Anyway. You're better at kicking down doors. You're better at jumping out of windows, but...

ALBERTO   But what?

PAULINA   That kid is capable of being utterly devoted to her. Truly devoted, do you understand?

ALBERTO   That kid is a homosexual, Paulina. I can smell them. Seriously. Homosexuals who don't know they're homosexuals have a very particular smell: like apples.

PAULINA   That's right, like apples.

ALBERTO   They do, don't they?

PAULINA   But all young virgins smell like
           apples, Alberto.

ALBERTO   The only thing I know is that I
           want to wake up next to her each
           morning. Have breakfast with
           her. Look at the goddamned
           rings under her eyes. Paulina,
           listen to me: she needs me too.
           She needs a man who's mature,
           intelligent, with imagination,
           who will help her grow — aren't I
           right? Say I'm right. Please.

PAULINA   (She takes his hands. Intimate,
           affectionate) No, no, Alberto. I'm
           going to beg you to stop being
           such a cliché. Please. The problem
           is that you can't stand losing,
           that's all. Losing with a whimper.

ALBERTO   Losing with a whimper?

PAULINA   We always prefer to go out with a
           bang. By our own choice. Losing
           makes us sad. Losing is bad for
           our health. But there's a certain

dignity that always comes from defeat. A certain nobility that emerges. When we lose or we get sick, that which makes us survive, that primal impulse, that cosmic will which makes us survive in spite of everything, reveals itself in us. And when it revealed itself in <u>you</u>, you went to enroll in Transcendental Meditation, isn't that right? But you didn't like the atmosphere.

ALBERTO   That guru was wearing a necklace and had hair down to here *(indicates his shoulders)* and a rose in his hand. He was fucking holding a rose.

PAULINA   What you need is to stop <u>worrying</u> about your destiny and to start <u>dealing</u> with it.

ALBERTO   Stop worrying and start dealing... What do you mean?

PAULINA   *(Caressing his cheek)* By breaking with the past. By giving yourself over to what comes along. By looking at the present. The past is past, Alberto. You have to look at what's in front of you. Right before your eyes.

PAULINA and ALBERTO exchange a long look. PAULINA touches ALBERTO'S shoulders.

ALBERTO   They're tense.

PAULINA   Like rock.

PAULINA massages his shoulders.

ALBERTO   *(Sighs)* I...

PAULINA   Shhh... *(She keeps massaging)* Better?

ALBERTO   Better.

PAULINA   Good. Relax. Let your arms flop. *(They both stop. PAULINA takes his hands and shakes out his arms.)* Let them go, nice and loose. Put your arms around me.

ALBERTO is dubious.

ALBERTO   It's just that I don't know you.

PAULINA   I'm going to crack your spine. *(ALBERTO hugs her. She cracks him three times.)* Sit down. *(They sit.)* Now your hands. *(She massages his hands. He cries out in pain)*

PAULINA   Breathe, breathe. They're pressure points. Relax. I'm waiting for you to relax.

ALBERTO   The truth is, I—I don't know what to do with myself. The thing with Gina, finishing the Villa book too. I was left without any life plan. These days we don't have any living heros in our midst; the revolution is dead, it was YOUR GRANDFATHER who killed the 1910 revolution. *(Paulina touches another pressure point and he cries out in pain.)*

PAULINA   Breathe, breathe. Breathe.

ALBERTO   And the revolution my
           generation promised didn't even
           happen. So you're right, "I'm
           weighed down by mediocrity."
           I'm weighed down by seeing the
           bunch of crooks in power today. I
           don't know where I ever got the
           idea the world could be fair, and
           not the web of pettiness and
           indecency I've spent the last
           fifteen years denouncing in the
           newspaper. I'm exhausted, Gina.

PAULINA   Paulina.

ALBERTO   Paulina.

The massage is over. PAULINA shakes her hands
           out vigorously.

PAULINA   You had some really bad energy.

(A beat)

ALBERTO   You know something? You really
           look like President Calles.

PAULINA   Why shouldn't I? I'm his
           granddaughter.

ALBERTO   But in this light, even more so. It
           gives you weird shadows.
           *(Touching her face with his index
           finger.)* Around your eyes, for
           example, so that your eyes seem
           blacker. Almost like onyx. Like
           small pieces of onyx, bluish black,
           like his. And on your upper lip,
           that is, above your upper lip, you
           have another shadow, and it
           looks like you have—just like the
           President—a little moustache.

PAULINA   Seriously?

ALBERTO   A little moustache.

*ALBERTO traces the location of the moustache
           with his index finger.*

PAULINA   *(tenderly kisses him on the neck)*
           Listen Alberto, why don't you
           write about Elías Calles? I'm
           serious.

ALBERTO   About your grandfather?

PAULINA   I have his personal archives here,
           in the bedroom. Since I'm the
           youngest grandchild, and I didn't
           know him well, I'm the one who
           inherited them.

ALBERTO   Along with some property too, I
           suppose.

PAULINA   Of course, of course. There are
           some rather surprising
           unpublished papers. There are
           documents that were secret in his
           time. It would be a revealing
           book.

ALBERTO   No. I'd make mincemeat of your
           grandfather. Goddamed
           nepotistic bourgeois corrupting
           fucking sonofabitch nation-seller.
           I'd reduce him to a pile of shit.

PAULINA   I don't think it would matter to
           him. He's already a pile of ashes.
           (*PAULINA goes to the bookcase and
           searches among the books. She takes*

*out the book about Villa. She opens
it.)* I'm going to quote you. I have
it marked with a silver bookmark
and underlined with yellow
highlighter. *(She turns on the tape
player with a kick. Music plays.)*
"Plutarco Elías Calles epitomized
the middle class's betrayal of the
popular revolution led by Pancho
Villa and Emiliano Zapata."

ALBERTO   So it says.

PAULINA   That's quite a sentence.

ALBERTO   Well it's true, even if it's not
           brilliantly written.

PAULINA   Show me.

ALBERTO   Pardon me?

PAULINA   Show me. You know what I
           mean. Do research, organize my
           grandfather's private papers, and
           prove it. In writing.

121

ALBERTO   Ha. All right. *(He laughs quietly. He moves close to her.)* Ha. The little moustache.

PAULINA kisses him on the lips, briefly.

ALBERTO   Ha.

PAULINA kisses him again, at length.

The tip of a cannon enters from offstage.

ALBERTO   Maybe. Why not? Maybe.

Suddenly ALBERTO stands up and scoops PAULINA up in his arms. He carries her to the bedroom. The entire cannon is now onstage, with Villa sitting on the base.

SCENE 2

VILLA turns the crank to extend the shaft of the cannon. It is immense, telescoping out to extend across the whole stage. VILLA lights the cannon's wick: it fires, but the tip of the cannon falls to the ground.

PAULINA enters from the bedroom, wearing the silk dressing gown we had seen on Gina earlier. She is irritated. She is even more annoyed by the little ball that falls out of the cannon and bounces around. She goes to the bar to pour two glasses of cognac.

SCENE 3

ALBERTO, comes back into the living room, carrying his shoes and socks.

A beat.

ALBERTO   I... couldn't... and I think that... I think that... for a while... I won't be able to... *(He stands and walks to the door)*...I won't be able to... forget her.

ALBERTO exits.
PAULINA remains alone, a glass of cognac in each hand.

THE END

Made in the USA
Lexington, KY
07 January 2018